RICHARD III

Retold by Tony Bradman

Illustrated by Mark Oldroyd

A & C Black • London

First published 2009 by
A & C Black Publishers Ltd
36 Soho Square, London, W1D 3QY

www.acblack.com

ISBN 978 1 4081 0471 2

A CIP catalogue for this book is available from the British Library.

This book is produced using paper that is made from wood grown
in managed, sustainable forests. It is natural, renewable and
recyclable. The logging and manufacturing processes conform
to the environmental regulations of the country of origin.

Printed and bound in Great Britain
by CPI Cox & Wyman, Reading, RG1 8EX.

Contents

List of characters

King Edward IV
Edward, Prince of Wales, *son of King Edward*
Richard, Duke of York, *son of King Edward*
Richard, *King Edward's brother, later King Richard III*
Clarence, *King Edward's brother*
Henry, Earl of Richmond, *later King Henry VII*
Sir Robert Brakenbury, *Lieutenant of the Tower*
Elizabeth, *King Edward's wife*
Lord Rivers, *brother to Elizabeth*
Marquis of Dorset and Lord Grey, *sons of Elizabeth*
Lord Buckingham
Lord Stanley
Lord Hastings
Lord Derby
Lord Norfolk
Sir William Catesby
Sir Thomas Vaughan
Sir James Tyrrel
Sir Richard Ratcliffe
Captain Blunt

Archbishop of York

Lord Mayor of London

Duchess of York, *mother to King Edward*

Margaret, *widow of King Henry VI*

Lady Anne, *widow of the former Prince of Wales*

Edward and Margaret, *children of Clarence*

George, *son of Lord Derby*

Act One

Plots and Schemes

It was a fine day in London, the sun shining down on the happy crowds in the streets. There was much to celebrate – the long years of civil war were over at last, the terrible bloodletting at an end. The two great noble families of York and Lancaster had fought each other for the English crown in the Wars of the Roses – Lancaster's badge was a red rose, York's a white. And York had won.

Edward of York now ruled as King Edward the Fourth. He had captured his rival, Henry of Lancaster, and had him murdered in the Tower of London. The crowds danced beneath that grim castle's walls, forgetting that Henry had once been King Henry the Sixth. They thought of nothing but the better days to come.

Although not everyone was happy. A strange, hunchbacked man stood in the shadows near the doors of Edward's palace, watching the crowds with his eyes narrowed. Yet deformed as he was, the man carried a sword and looked like a soldier. For this was Richard, Duke of Gloucester, King Edward's brother...

'Now is the winter of our discontent,' Richard murmured, looking up at the blue sky, 'made glorious summer by this sun of York.'

He loved the clever use of words, and smiled at the pun. His brother Edward was the most popular *son* of the House of York. Because of Edward, the clouds of war that had hung over the country and the York family were gone, and they could all bask in the *sun* of peace. Edward had certainly enjoyed himself with his parties and dancing...

A girl in the crowd turned to glance at Richard, then hurriedly looked away. Richard's smile vanished. He knew what he was – a poor, misshapen creature, brought unfinished into this world, so ugly that dogs barked at him as he limped by. Well then, if he couldn't be a lover, he was determined to be a villain. He had nothing to keep him busy now the war was over, so he was plotting to make Edward hate their other brother, Clarence. Richard's smile returned as he thought of just how stupid and gullible his brothers were.

Suddenly, he heard the palace doors opening. Richard stepped from the shadows and saw Clarence being marched out with an escort of soldiers. Leading them was an officer called Brakenbury, Lieutenant of the Tower.

'Good day to you, brother,' said Richard. 'Why the armed guard?'

'The king is sending me to the Tower,' said a frightened Clarence.

'For what reason?' said Richard, his voice full of false concern.

'We both know he's been behaving strangely,' said Clarence. 'Well, now it seems he's heard a prophecy that someone with my name will steal his crown.'

'I blame his wife, Elizabeth, and her family,' Richard whispered, deciding to spread a little more poison. 'She puts evil thoughts in his mind. Why, she was the one who made Edward send Lord Hastings to the Tower. They're letting him out today, but I tell you, Clarence, none of us are safe at the moment.'

'I'm very sorry, my lord,' said Brakenbury, stepping forward. 'But the king gave me strict orders that no one was allowed to speak with Lord Clarence.'

'Is that right?' said Richard, pretending to be angry. 'Well, never mind. I know you've got your job to do, Brakenbury, so I'll let you go. Don't despair, Clarence, I'll get you out – I'll speak to Edward, I promise!'

Clarence was led off ... and the instant his brother was gone, Richard smiled a wicked smile. 'Farewell, Clarence,' he murmured. 'Ha! You won't be coming back from there any time soon. I love you so much, I'm about to send your soul to heaven...'

Just then Lord Hastings came round the

14

corner, and Richard hailed him.

'Welcome back, Lord Hastings!' he said. 'It's good to see you. But I'm sorry to report that my brother Clarence is taking your place in the Tower today. Those who plotted against you have now turned their attention to him.'

'We live in evil times,' said Hastings, shaking his head. 'And there may be worse to come. I've heard the king is sick, and his doctors fear for his life.'

'That is bad news,' murmured Richard, putting on a worried expression. 'Still, he brought it on himself with the kind of life he led. Is he in bed?'

Hastings said he was, and hurried off.

Richard stepped back into the shadows to think about this development. Of course, he wanted Edward to die, but not before Clarence. Which meant that he needed to work quickly on Edward, and trick him into disposing of Clarence soon. But that should be easy with the plan he had devised. And once they were both out of the way, many doors would be open to a bustling master of plots and schemes like him. Mind you, having a wife would be useful in his rise to power, too. One woman in particular seemed perfect. And here she was now...

A column of soldiers bearing a coffin came marching down the street. Leading them was a beautiful young woman, the Lady Anne. Richard knew the coffin contained the body of Henry of Lancaster. Lady Anne was the widow of Henry's son, the former Prince of Wales.

Richard smiled that wicked smile of his again. What did it matter that he was the man who had killed both her father and her husband? He would make up for it by marrying her. She would be quite a tough nut to crack, but it would probably be fun... Richard stepped out of the shadows and held up his hand.

The column halted and Anne glared at him. 'What magician has conjured this foul fiend to stop us?' she hissed. 'Get away from me, you devil! I curse you from the bottom of my heart, you spider, you toad, you venomous thing...'

'Please, my lady, don't be so cruel,' said Richard, smiling at her, turning on all his charm. He could be very charming when he wanted – or needed – to be.

'How dare you stand before this coffin, you foul lump of deformity!' yelled Anne. 'You're inhuman and unnatural and I wish that Heaven would strike you dead with a lightning bolt, or that the Earth would open up and swallow you!'

'Do you know, you're even more beautiful when you're angry...' said Richard. 'And I just wish you would give me a chance to explain myself. Maybe I *did* kill your father and your husband. But that was in a war, and it doesn't really matter now. I have something far more important to say... I can't stop thinking about you, Anne, and

I want you to become my wife.'

Anne spat in his face. Richard didn't blink, but simply wiped the spit away, and kept on talking and smiling. After a while, Anne began to calm down, and even seemed to warm to the strange-looking man in front of her. The coffin bearers could hardly believe what they were seeing. It was like watching a wizard practise his dark arts, a snake charmer hypnotising an unsuspecting cobra...

'Take my blade and kill me,' said Richard eventually. He made her hold his sword and knelt down, ripping open his shirt. 'I would rather die than lose you.'

'No... No...' murmured Anne. She was confused, and let the sword fall. 'Please stand up. I might have wanted you dead, but I will not be your executioner.'

'Very well, tell me to kill myself,' said Richard, picking up the sword.

'I wish I knew what was in your heart,' said Anne, staring into his eyes.

'No more than what's on my tongue,' said Richard, returning her gaze.

'I fear both are false...' said Anne. 'No matter, put your sword away.'

Richard did so, and smiled his wicked smile again. He knew he had won.

'Let me bury this noble king,' he said, pointing at the coffin. 'I'll wet his grave with tears of repentance, then come to see you, if I may. Please say yes.'

'With all my heart, although it's more than you deserve,' said Anne. 'But it gives me great joy to hear that you're sorry for what you've done... Farewell.'

Richard watched her go, then sent off the soldiers to bury Henry. Of course he didn't feel sorry for killing the king, and the instant he was alone he did a little dance of triumph. Anne had hated him, but they would be married – though she wouldn't be his wife for long. And in the meantime he should find out what was happening elsewhere...

Richard hurried into the palace and scuttled along its dark, winding passages, a spider searching for new prey. Presently he heard hushed voices, and he slipped into a pool of shadow where he couldn't be seen. He peered into a chamber, and saw Elizabeth, King Edward's wife. She was talking in worried whispers to Lord Rivers, her brother, and her two grown-up sons from a previous marriage, the Marquis of Dorset and Lord Grey. They were soon joined by two more lords, Buckingham and Stanley of Derby.

'Try to stay calm, sister,' said Rivers. 'I'm sure the king will recover.'

'But what if he doesn't?' said Elizabeth. 'What will happen to me then?'

'Nothing,' said Grey. 'Don't forget that you and the king have been blessed with two other sons. The oldest will be the new king, and you're his mother!'

'But he will be a child, and it's been

arranged that after Edward's death, Richard will be the new king's Lord Protector until he grows up,' said Elizabeth, biting her lip. 'And Richard is a man with no love for me, nor any of you.'

'Is that the kind of thing you say to the king about me?' hissed Richard, stepping out of the darkness. 'Well, I won't put up with your lies any more.'

'I'm only telling the truth,' said Elizabeth. 'I know you're jealous of me...'

An argument began, with Richard blaming Elizabeth for what had happened to both Hastings and Clarence. Elizabeth and her family and friends denied it, but voices were raised, and Richard kept on at them, needling and goading.

Suddenly, an older woman appeared from the doorway, her hair wild and her rich clothes torn and dirty. It was Margaret, the widow of Henry of Lancaster. Everyone instantly fell silent and stared at her.

'How typical!' yelled Margaret. 'You were snarling at each other, but as soon as I arrive, you all turn your hatred on me! You are the cause of my misery...'

'Oh please, spare us the complaints, you withered hag,' growled Richard.

'Foul shame on you!' wailed Margaret. 'And you, and you, and you,' she added, pointing at the others one by one. 'This dog, this son of hell, might have done the killing, but you were all part of it, you vile traitors, and I curse you. But mark my words, you can't trust him. He'll be the death of you, I swear!'

Margaret ranted on and on, until finally someone came to lead her away.

'I wish I hadn't spoken so harshly,' said Richard, trying to look as if he felt guilty, and not succeeding. 'I'm sorry for the part I played in her troubles...'

At that moment an attendant of the king arrived, a certain Sir William Catesby.

'Majesty, the king has asked to see you,' he said to Elizabeth.

The chamber emptied of everybody except Richard. He had managed to persuade Edward to have Clarence executed. Edward had afterwards changed his mind, but Richard had ignored the message that would have saved Clarence's life. Instead he had arranged to meet two men with special skills...

'Ah, here come my sturdy executioners,' he whispered as the men emerged from the shadows of the passage beyond. 'Are you going to do the job for me?'

'We are, my lord,' said the first man. Both were dark and burly and had mean faces. 'But we need a pass from you so they'll let us into the Tower.'

'Quite right, too,' said Richard, handing the man a scroll. 'Remember, do it quickly, and don't let him speak. He's quite capable of making you pity him.'

23

'Don't worry,' said the man. 'We won't chat. Talkers aren't good doers.'

'Marvellous, straight to it...' said Richard. 'I like you lads. Off you go!'

Richard left them and cheerfully went about his business of plotting and creating mayhem wherever he could, while they made for the Tower. Richard's pass got them in ... and soon the door to Clarence's dark and dingy dungeon creaked open. He was asleep, but woke when their shadows fell across him.

'Is that you, jail keeper?' he mumbled, distracted. 'Give me a cup of wine.'

'You'll have plenty of wine soon enough,' said the first murderer. 'We'll use our knives,' he whispered, 'then drown him in that barrel outside...'

The second murderer just nodded, and suddenly Clarence realised something was very wrong. He went pale, and scrambled away from them, into a corner. 'How deadly you look!' he said. 'Have you come to kill me?'

'We have,' said the murderers, advancing on him, knives raised.

'Wait!' Clarence said desperately. 'Send a message to my brother Richard. He'll reward you better for my life than Edward will for news of my death.'

'You're a fool,' said the first murderer. 'It's *Richard* who wants you dead.'

The two murderers got on with their dirty work, and soon Clarence's royal blood was mingled with the jail keeper's cheap wine.

Richard heard the good news at the end of the day. One brother was gone, but another still left in his way...

Act Two

Mothers and Sons

The sick King Edward lay in his great royal bed, surrounded by his family, counsellors, attendants, and many doctors.

'Every day I expect to be summoned to Heaven,' he said. 'And my soul will be more at peace there if I know I have made my friends at peace on Earth... I want you all to swear that you will be friends with each other from now on.'

The chamber was full of people who had been in bitter conflict throughout the civil war. Most of them were organised in groups and were still plotting. But now they did as the dying king wished, or at least made a public show of it. Elizabeth made up with Hastings, and Buckingham and Rivers and Dorset and Grey swore eternal friendship with anybody who had ever been their enemy.

'This is wonderful medicine for my sickly heart,' said King Edward. 'All we need is for my brother Richard to add his voice to these promises. Where is he?'

Just then Richard limped into the royal bedchamber, smiling and nodding.

'Good day, good day!' he said. 'I'm pleased to see such a happy gathering!'

'Well, it's no wonder we're happy,' said Edward. 'We've spent our time doing happy things. I've made everyone agree to be friends from now on.'

'I'm so glad to hear it,' Richard declared, and put on a solemn expression. 'Well, I too would like to say I'm sorry if anybody here thinks I am their enemy because of some false rumour, or if I've ever said anything to upset them.'

Everybody started clapping, the applause followed by a general round of handshakes and hearty hugs and much backslapping. Edward simply beamed.

'I think this should be a holy day in future,' said Elizabeth. 'And to make our joy complete, my dear husband, I beg you to forgive Clarence and free him.'

Richard looked shocked, and recoiled from her in disgust. An uneasy silence descended on the chamber as people saw his reaction. 'Is that some kind of sick joke, my lady?' he growled. 'My brother Clarence is dead. I thought everybody in the palace knew that.'

There were gasps of surprise and horror around them.

'Well, I didn't,' said Edward. What little colour he had was draining from his cheeks, leaving him deathly pale. 'I'm sure I reversed the execution order!'

'You might have done, my lord,' Richard said, looking as sad as he could. 'But it was your first order that was followed. The second must have come too late. I only hope nobody here was to blame for the messenger being so slow.' He glared at Elizabeth and her family, and suddenly the chamber was filled with muttering and dark looks.

Some people made it obvious they were on Richard's side, Buckingham among them.

Richard turned and whispered to him.

'Did you see how pale Elizabeth went when she heard that Clarence was dead?' he said. 'I'll bet she and her family put the idea in the king's mind in the first place...'

'Why did no one speak up for poor Clarence?' Edward moaned. His doctors clustered round, and it was clear he was taking a turn for the worse. 'He was a good brother to me, and yet I had him killed. I'll pay for this crime, I'm sure...'

Richard quietly slipped out of the king's chamber, pleased with another day's evil work. Things were going brilliantly. People were whispering in dark corners all over London, worried about what was going on. None of them seemed to realise that they were caught in Richard's web of intrigue, his plan to become king...

In another part of the palace, Richard's mother, the Duchess of York, was weeping and calling out Clarence's name. Two of her grandchildren were with her, Clarence's son and daughter.

'My uncle the king is to blame for my father's death,' muttered the boy, whose name was also Edward. 'I'll pray to God to take revenge on him for it.'

'So will I,' said his sister, whose name was Margaret.

'Hush now, children,' said the Duchess of York, hugging them to her. 'The king loves you, and you mustn't think it was his fault. You're young and innocent and you have no idea who really caused your father's death.'

'But we do!' said the boy. 'My good uncle Richard told me the queen persuaded the king to kill our father. Then Uncle Richard cried and told us we were to think of *him* as our father now, and that he would take care of us.'

'Oh, did he?' murmured the Duchess of York. Richard was her son, but she had no illusions about him. She knew he was full of dark deceit and trickery.

'Do you think he was telling us the truth, grandmother?' said Edward.

'No, boy, I do not,' said the Duchess of York. 'But wait, who is this?'

Queen Elizabeth had suddenly come running into the chamber. She looked terrible, her hair unpinned and wild, her face pale, and tears streaming down her cheeks. Rivers and Dorset came in, too, trailing unhappily along behind her.

'The king is dead!' she wailed, throwing herself down before the duchess. 'I wish that I could die, too, and hurry after his soul as it flies towards Heaven!'

'No, no!' moaned the duchess. 'I wept when my husband died, but this is worse. Two sons I've lost, two copies of their father smashed by death. And the only son that's left is a warped copy, one that grieves me when I see it...'

Rivers pulled Elizabeth up from the floor.

'Sister, think of your son, the Prince of Wales,' he whispered urgently. 'Send for him now and have him crowned king as soon as possible.' The Prince of Wales had been sent away to Ludlow, in the country, for his safety. 'He will be our best, our only protection.'

Elizabeth had no time to reply, for at that moment Richard swept into the room. With him were Buckingham, Derby, Hastings and others. More and more people had realised Richard's power was growing, and were joining his group. To them it seemed the safest thing to do.

'Calm yourself, Elizabeth,' said Richard, smiling at her. 'We are all stricken with grief, but weeping won't help. Oh, hello, Mother – I didn't see you there.'

'God bless you, my son,' snapped the Duchess of York. 'And I hope he puts meekness, and love, and charity, and a true sense of duty in your heart.'

'Amen to that!' Richard said loudly, and

rolled his eyes at his friends. He nudged Buckingham, who stepped forward to make a general announcement.

'It's time for us to stop grieving,' he said. 'We must fetch the young prince here to be crowned – but without too many soldiers in his escort, of course.'

'Really? May I ask why that is?' said Rivers, his voice full of suspicion. Having the Prince of Wales brought to London was a good thing. But the idea of only giving him a small escort seemed dangerous, even threatening in some way. Rivers and Dorset exchanged a look, and behind them Elizabeth frowned.

'Because we don't want to worry anybody,' Buckingham said smoothly. 'The war hasn't been over long. If people saw a great column of soldiers heading for London, it might make them think there was going to be trouble of some sort. After all, everybody knows that many of us were arguing until just recently.'

'Well, I very much hope we're going to keep the promises we made to the late king,' said Richard. 'I intend to, anyway. What about the rest of you?'

'Oh yes, without a doubt,' said Rivers, everybody else quickly murmuring their agreement. No one wanted to be seen as an oath-breaker, someone who couldn't be trusted. 'Good point, Buckingham,' Rivers continued. 'We wouldn't want to cause any, er ... anxiety. I agree – not too many soldiers in the escort.'

'Good, I'm glad that's settled,' said Richard, smiling. 'I'd love to stay and chat, but I'm afraid I've got a lot of rather important business to take care of.'

He left the chamber with Buckingham. They hurried through the corridors of the palace until they found a secluded corner where no one would hear them.

'You and I should go to fetch the young prince,' whispered Buckingham.

'And we definitely need to keep Elizabeth's family well away from him.'

'That's good advice,' Richard whispered. 'Let's head for Ludlow...'

News of King Edward's death spread round the country like fire in a field of straw. It didn't matter that the Prince of Wales had only a small escort, people had heard rumours, and were worried already. 'Woe to the land that is governed by a child!' said many, and few people really trusted Richard.

Not that anyone particularly trusted Elizabeth and her family. Her sons and brother were thought to be proud and arrogant, and almost guaranteed to cause conflict of some kind. So the hearts of England's people were full of dread. When great leaves fall, they said, then winter is surely on its way again...

A few days later, Richard's mother was in her chamber at the palace, waiting for news.

With her were Elizabeth and the youngest of the queen's sons, the brother of the Prince of Wales. The boy had a title – Duke of York. Strangely enough, he too was called Richard, and his brother was another Edward. But the people had their own name for them – the Little Princes.

At last the door opened and a servant ushered in a richly dressed man of the church. It was the Archbishop of York, a friend and supporter of the duchess.

'My lady, I've heard that the prince and his escort are at Northampton tonight,' he said. 'So he'll be here tomorrow, or the next day at the latest.'

'I'm longing to see him,' said the duchess. 'I'll bet he's grown so much!'

'Ah, but I've been told he hasn't,' said Elizabeth, smiling at her son. 'In fact, it seems that the Duke of York here has almost caught up with his brother.'

'That's true,' said the young Duke of

York, sighing. 'But I wish it wasn't.'

'Why do you say such a thing?' asked the duchess. 'It's good to grow!'

'Well, at dinner the other night, Uncle Rivers was talking about how I'm growing faster than my brother,' the boy answered. 'Then Uncle Richard said that sweet flowers grow slowly, and only weeds grow fast. People don't like weeds, do they? So I think I'd rather be like a sweet flower, and grow slowly.'

'He's a fine one to talk,' muttered the duchess. 'He took an awfully long time to grow. So by his rule he should be the sweetest flower of them all...'

'And so he is I'm sure, my lady,' said the archbishop, crossing himself.

'Yes, well, I'll be the judge of that,' said the duchess. 'I'm his mother.'

Suddenly, they heard footsteps in the passage outside, and a messenger hurried in. The duchess and Elizabeth glanced at each other. They knew instantly from the man's expression that he had come to give them bad news.

'Lord Rivers and Lord Grey have been arrested, and so has Sir Thomas Vaughan,' said the messenger. 'They've all been sent to Pomfret Castle.'

Sir Thomas Vaughan was another member of Elizabeth's group, and Pomfret Castle was the kind of place that prisoners seldom came out of alive. The messenger said they had been arrested on the orders of the two lords who were the mightiest men in the kingdom now – Richard and Buckingham. The duchess and Queen Elizabeth were horrified, their faces stricken with worry.

'What are the charges against them?' said the archbishop, his face grim.

'Er ... nobody seems to know, my lord,' said the messenger, shrugging.

'Oh no, I see nothing but ruin ahead!' groaned Elizabeth. 'There will be blood and destruction again. The shadow of a tyrant is falling over us.'

'How many days of war and terror have I seen?' moaned the duchess. 'Will it never be over? I wish I was dead, then I wouldn't have to see it all again!'

But Elizabeth was already thinking about the safety of her son. 'Come, my boy,' she said. 'We'll take sanctuary in the church. Farewell, Duchess.'

'Wait, I'll come with you!' said the duchess, and they hurried off.

The archbishop followed them as night fell swiftly on the city. Soft whispers filled its darkened streets, and rumours flew like bats across the shadowed land. The web of intrigue grew ever faster, spun from a venomous spider's hand...

Act Three

Off With His Head!

In London, a crowd had gathered outside the Tower to see the Prince of Wales arrive. Trumpets blared as the column trotted towards the gates, the young prince sitting proudly on his pony at their head. Beside him rode his uncle Richard and Buckingham, and behind them were the grim-faced soldiers of the escort, hardened men whose hands were never far from their sword hilts.

At last they came to a halt in the shadow of the walls. Richard dismounted, and smiled as Catesby – who was now his man – helped the prince from his pony. The crowd cheered the prince – too loudly, as far as Richard was concerned. Lord Hastings was at the gates, with other worthies from the city.

'I bid you welcome to your capital, dearest nephew!' said Richard, limping across to loom over the boy. 'Are you quite all right? You look rather sad.'

'Yes, Uncle, I'm fine,' said the prince, glancing up at him and the Tower's walls.

More of Richard's grim-faced soldiers peered down from the battlements. 'But I do wish my other uncle and my oldest brother were here to meet me.'

Buckingham scowled, and a ripple of muttering passed through the crowd. The prince was obviously talking about the imprisoned lords, Rivers and Grey.

'Ah, so young, so innocent!' said Richard, laughing, and not at all bothered – or at least that's the way he appeared. He ruffled the boy's golden hair. 'They're dangerous men, nephew. They seem nice but, believe me, they have poison in their evil hearts. God keep you from them, and from all such false friends!'

'But they're not false...' said the prince, puzzled.

Richard simply shrugged, and changed the subject. The prince asked after his mother and his youngest brother, and it was explained that the queen had taken sanctuary in a church.

'It's all rather unnecessary,' said Buckingham. 'Lord Hastings, I wonder if you wouldn't mind asking her to let the prince's brother come and see him.'

Hastings nodded and scurried off.

The young prince turned to Richard. 'Tell me, Uncle,' he said. 'Where am I staying until I'm crowned king?'

'Why, wherever you like,' said Richard. 'But if I may advise you, I would suggest the Tower. I think it would be far the best place for your, er ... health.'

'I don't like it at all,' said the prince. 'Wasn't it built by Julius Caesar?'

'Yes, I believe he began it,' said Richard, and closed his ears as the prince prattled on. He thought of the old saying about those who are clever when they're young not living long, and smiled his wicked smile secretly to himself.

The other prince arrived not long after, and the two brothers were pleased to be together once more. The Prince of Wales relaxed, and the boys were cheeky to their uncle Richard, poking fun at him. The crowd laughed and applauded their jokes. Richard soon saw how popular they could become with the people, and his black heart hardened against them even more. Not that he let it show.

'My dearest nephews, would you like to go inside now?' he said at last.

'What, into the Tower?' said the Duke of York. 'Do we have to? I'm afraid of my uncle Clarence's ghost. Grandmother told me he was murdered there.'

'Well, I'm not afraid of any dead relatives!' said the Prince of Wales.

'I hope you're not afraid of any living ones, either,' snapped Richard.

They looked at each other for a moment, the boy and his Lord Protector. Then the prince sighed again, and took his brother by the hand. The two boys went through the shadow of the great gatehouse and into the Tower. And to some people there, it seemed as if they were being swallowed up by darkness...

Richard stood for a while deep in thought, stroking his chin, his eyes fixed on the crowd. At last he nodded to Buckingham, who brought Catesby over.

'Well, Catesby,' said Buckingham, being careful not to let anyone overhear, 'you've sworn to help us, and also to keep quiet about what we ask you to do. You know what we're most interested in. Do you think we can persuade Lord Hastings to declare for Lord Richard here – and help him take the throne?'

'I'm not sure,' said Catesby, shaking his head. 'We could try, I suppose.'

'And what about Lord Derby?' said Buckingham. 'Whose side is he on?'

'Hard to tell,' said Catesby. 'But he'll back whoever Hastings supports.'

'Good,' whispered Buckingham, glancing

at Richard, who raised an eyebrow. 'Very well, go and sound out Hastings – carefully – then come back and report to us.'

'Tell him I'm having Rivers, Grey and Vaughan executed tomorrow,' said Richard. 'They're enemies of his, so it might make him think warmly of me.'

'I'll do as you ask, my lords,' said Catesby, and he slipped into the crowd.

'What shall we do if Hastings doesn't join us?' whispered Buckingham.

'Chop off his head!' said Richard, and laughed. 'But you'll have your reward for helping me, Buckingham. I'll make you rich when I am King.'

'Thank you, my lord,' said Buckingham, grinning. 'I'll look forward to it.'

'Yes, indeed, you'll get what you deserve,' said Richard, slapping him on the back. 'Let's have some supper. Plotting is a lot easier on a full stomach!'

Catesby came back with a full report on Lord Hastings later that same night. It appeared that Hastings was a firm supporter of the Prince of Wales. As far as he was concerned, there could be no other king. Derby agreed, but seemed less certain of the right thing to do, and Richard wondered if he might be able to twist him to his will... But Hastings was finished, a dead man walking.

Rivers, Grey and Vaughan were executed at Pomfret early the next morning, as Richard had ordered. Their heads were struck off, and stuck on poles to decorate the castle's battlements.

A week later, Richard invited the great men of the land to a dinner in the palace. Hastings and Buckingham were there to welcome them.

'My lords, we're here today to make a decision about the coronation,' said Hastings. 'I believe that everything is ready. We just need to choose the date.'

'Tomorrow would be good,' said a bishop, others murmuring in agreement.

'Does anyone know what the Lord Protector thinks?' asked Buckingham.

'Not really,' said Hastings, smiling. 'But the Duke of Gloucester looks like the cat that's got the cream this morning. But then we all know he's an easy man to read. His face always reveals what's in his heart.'

Most of the men in the dining hall looked at Hastings as if he was mad, but nobody said a word. For just then the doors flew open and Richard limped in. Behind him tramped a dozen soldiers in full armour, swords drawn.

Richard came to a halt, his dark eyes narrowed, his deadly gaze scanning the room.

'I have a question for you,' he said quietly, his voice full of menace. 'If someone used witchcraft in a plot against me, what would they deserve?'

'As a man who loves you dearly, my lord,

let me give you the answer,' said Hastings. 'It's a very simple one, too. Such a person would deserve death.'

'Well, it has happened,' yelled Richard. 'See what that witch Elizabeth's done! My arm is withered...' He pulled back his sleeve and held up his arm. Many of the people there thought it looked all right, that it was no more withered than it had ever been. But nobody argued with him.

Nobody, that is, except Hastings.

'Are you sure, my lord?' he said. 'If they have actually done anything...'

'*If?*' screamed Richard. 'It must be *you* who has bewitched me, then! Guards, off with this traitor's head! I swear I won't sit down to dinner until it's done...'

Hastings was dragged away groaning and begging for his life, but there was to be no mercy for him. To the horror of the assembled great men, moments later a soldier returned to the dining hall carrying his severed head.

The soldier placed it on the table in front of Richard, who put on an expression of sadness.

'Ah, I loved Hastings so much I feel like weeping!' he said. 'I took him for a straightforward, honest man, but he betrayed me... Now, what's for dinner?'

Hastings's head was taken away, but the meal was a rather quiet affair, the great men subdued and very nervous, nobody daring to mention the coronation of the new king. It was plain to see that most of them now feared for their own safety, and thought that worse was probably to come. Richard's mood was restored, though, and he ate and drank cheerfully, laughing and joking with Buckingham.

When the dinner was over and the last of the great men had scurried away, grateful to be alive, Richard and Buckingham talked about what to do next.

'I think it's time to spread a few rumours,' said Richard. 'We need to trash some reputations – my brother Edward's, of course, but it would also be good to change the way people think about those two awful brats of his. I don't mind what you say, just try to make them sound as nasty and unpleasant as possible.'

'I'll see to it immediately,' said Buckingham. 'You can rely on me, my lord.'

Richard smiled, and called Catesby to him again. He gave orders for security to be tightened at the Tower. Nobody was to be allowed to see the Little Princes without his express permission, not even their mother. In fact, *especially* not their mother, he thought, determined to destroy Elizabeth and all her group...

The weeks went by, and bit by bit, supporter by supporter, Richard increased his power. Buckingham worked on the great men, the lords and the bishops and the archbishops. He talked endlessly about Richard's wisdom and his strength and courage in war – and what a wonderful king such a man would make. And one day, a group of great men asked if they could visit Richard at the palace.

'What do you think, Buckingham?' said Richard. 'How do we handle this?'

'I'm pretty sure they're going to offer you the crown,' said Buckingham. 'But I don't think you should accept it straightaway. You should play hard to get.'

'Yes, I like it!' said Richard, laughing. 'It never pays to seem too eager.'

And so Richard and Buckingham worked out a whole performance. When the great men arrived, led by the Lord Mayor of London, they were shown to the Royal Audience Chamber with its empty throne. They asked to see the Lord Protector, and Catesby was sent to give him the message. But the answer was that the Lord Protector was busy praying to God and meditating with two priests, and that he would not be able to see anyone until the following day.

'Go back and ask him again, Catesby,' said Buckingham, 'and tell him that we have something very important to discuss with him – the fate of our nation!'

'Your wish is my command,' said Catesby with a wink, and scampered off.

'You see, my lords!' said Buckingham, turning to the assembled great men. 'Richard is nothing like his brother Edward. Richard isn't going to parties and drinking too much. No, he is a good man. England would be such a happy place if he agreed to be our king. But I'm not sure we'll be able to convince him.'

'Oh, I hope you're wrong,' the Lord Mayor said hurriedly, all the great men there agreeing with him.

At last the doors swung open and Richard entered. He was flanked by two bishops, with Catesby and a dozen soldiers behind them.

'Good morning, my lords,' said Richard. 'Forgive me for not wanting to speak to you at first, but as you can see, I was busy serving my god. Still, I'm here now, so perhaps you can tell me about this important matter of yours.'

'My lord, I think I can speak for us all here,' said Buckingham, going down on one knee. 'We heartily beg you to be our king. It is your right, by birth.'

'How can you say that?' Richard murmured. 'There is another who has more right than me. Of course he's very young, but he'll be old enough one day...'

Buckingham begged to differ, and so did the Lord Mayor and many of the great men. They said Richard had every right to be their monarch, and pleaded with him. Richard shook his head, saying he wasn't ready to be King and take on the burdens of state. Buckingham wouldn't let the subject drop, and at one point Richard pretended to lose his temper. He ordered them all out, and had to be persuaded to let them return. That's what Catesby said, anyway. In fact, he and Richard had burst into fits of giggles when they were left on their own.

At last Richard allowed them back into the Audience Chamber. He stood by the throne, and they gathered silently in front of him, waiting for him to speak.

'Very well, I accept,' he said. 'But I want everybody to know that I never, ever wanted this. I'm only doing it because you have forced me to say yes.'

'Then I salute you with this royal title!' cried Buckingham, raising his sword. 'Long live King Richard the Third, England's worthy king! Hip hip – hooray!'

The whole palace rang with cheers. Richard sat on the throne and smiled his wicked smile, but it soon faded. He stopped listening, and his mind drifted to a cell in the Tower. So long as they lived, those brats were a threat to his power...

Act Four

A Mother's Curse

ACT FOUR

That very same day, three women were heading for the Tower – Richard's mother, the Duchess of York, his wife, the Lady Anne, and the former queen, Lady Elizabeth. With them was Elizabeth's older son, Dorset. They stopped in the shadow of the great gatehouse and Elizabeth knocked on a small side door. It opened at last, and out came the Lieutenant of the Tower, Brakenbury.

'Good morning, Brakenbury,' said Elizabeth. 'How are my sons?'

'Er … very well, my lady,' murmured Brakenbury, an embarrassed look on his face. 'But I'm afraid I can't let you in at the moment. The king has given strict orders that you're not allowed to see them. None of you are, in fact.'

'The king?' said Elizabeth, looking puzzled. 'Who do you mean?'

'I mean the Lord Protector,' said Brakenbury. 'He is the new king.'

'He can't be!' said Elizabeth, horrified. The other two women exchanged worried looks. 'And he can't stop me seeing my children – I'm their mother!'

'And I'm their grandmother,' said the duchess. 'I *insist* on seeing them!'

'And I'm their aunt,' said Lady Anne. 'I'll have you sacked for this!'

'You must do as you wish,' said Brakenbury. 'Good day to you, ladies.'

He went back inside and closed the door. Just then Lord Derby arrived.

'My Lady Anne, your husband has sent me to fetch you,' he said. 'You're wanted in Westminster – you are to be crowned as Richard's royal queen.'

'I'll come with you, Derby,' Anne said quietly. 'Although I go with a heavy heart. Being married to Richard has been a nightmare. He needed a wife, so he tricked me with his honeyed words. And no doubt he'll shortly be rid of me.'

'Are you all right, Mother?' said Dorset, concerned by the look on her face.

'You shouldn't waste your time worrying about me,' Elizabeth said, gripping his arm. 'You must get away as soon as you can! Richard hates us, so if you want to stay alive, leave this slaughterhouse and go to the Earl of Richmond.'

Henry, Earl of Richmond, was a distant descendant of another former king, Edward the Third, and that gave him a claim to the throne. Henry was in France, keeping out of Richard's way, but now a rumour had been spreading that he was going to invade England to depose Richard. Many people hoped it was true. Richard had proved himself to be a tyrant, and people were starting to hate him.

'That's good advice,' said Derby, carefully looking over his shoulder, making sure none of Richard's spies were listening.

Derby's wife had been married before,

and Richmond was her oldest son – which made things difficult for Derby. He and his wife had a grown-up son of their own called George, who was a supporter of his half-brother. Now Derby said that George would help Dorset get to Richmond, and agreed to write a letter for Dorset to give him.

'Time for you all to leave, I think,' said Derby at last, and they turned to go.

'Wait just a moment,' said Elizabeth, anxiously looking back at the Tower. 'You rough stones, have pity for my tender babies, locked inside your walls...' she sighed, and they hurried off in different directions.

Richard and Anne were crowned later that morning, but he didn't enjoy the great feast laid on for him afterwards. He sent Anne to her chamber and sat darkly brooding, barely listening to the chatter around him and the loyal toasts proposed in his name. At last he crooked his little finger to summon Buckingham to his side.

'It's time for me to see how truly loyal you are, Buckingham,' he whispered. 'The Little Princes still live. Now … can you guess what I want to say to you?'

'Tell me, my lord,' said Buckingham. He had a bad feeling about this.

'Why, Buckingham,' said Richard, his eyes narrowed. 'I want to be King.'

'You are already, my lord,' said Buckingham. 'You've been crowned…'

'But I can't be sure of my throne yet, can I?' hissed Richard, beginning to lose his temper. 'Come on, Buckingham, you're not usually this slow. Do I have to spell it out for you? I want both the brats dead, and I want it done as quickly as possible. What do you say to that, eh? Are you with me in this?'

'Well, you must do as you think fit,' Buckingham murmured uneasily. The murder of two children was an outrage too far, even for a man like him. 'Er … let me think about it. I'll give you an answer later.'

Buckingham quickly left the feast, his head down. Richard watched him go, then turned to Catesby, who stood behind him. Catesby leaned in close to him.

'Send for that man you told me about,' Richard whispered. 'I'll see him now. Oh, and by the way, I want you to start spreading a rumour that the Lady Anne is very sick. That way people won't be so surprised when she dies suddenly...'

Richard was still spinning plots, trying to make his web stronger. He would need another wife once he had got rid of Anne, one who had better connections to the royal line – his brother Clarence's daughter, Margaret. Yes, he thought, murder the Little Princes, then marry the girl when she was old enough. That was the way to do it, even if it did mean more evil. But what did that matter? He was so deep in blood and sin that a little more made no difference.

Once the feast was over, Richard went to his private chamber. Catesby was waiting for him with a shifty-looking man in poor clothes. It was evening, and the candles in the room made pools of light in the darkness, and cast strange, flickering shadows on their faces. Richard nodded, and Catesby slipped out.

'James Tyrrel, my lord...' said the man. 'Your most obedient subject.'

'Are you really?' said Richard.

Tyrrel remained steady under his gaze. 'Try me,' he said, and Richard limped over to stand close beside him.

'Are you willing to kill ... a friend of mine?' Richard whispered in his ear.

'If you like,' Tyrrel said calmly. 'But I'd rather kill two of your enemies.'

'Good answer,' said Richard, stepping back from him. 'And I do have a couple of enemies I want you to deal with – those brats in the Tower.'

Richard promised to reward Tyrrel for his evil work, and the murderer was soon on his way to do the deed.

A little later, Buckingham came to see Richard. 'My lord, I've been thinking about what you asked me earlier,' he said nervously, his face pale in the soft candlelight.

Richard frowned at him. 'Forget it,' he said. 'Did you know that Dorset has fled to Richmond?'

'I did, my lord,' said Buckingham. 'But there was something else I wanted to talk to you about as well. I'd, er … like to claim that reward you promised me.'

'I remember Henry the Sixth prophesied that Richmond would be King one day,' Richard muttered, suddenly preoccupied by dark thoughts. 'At the time Richmond was just an irritating little boy. I should have killed the pest then…'

'My lord,' said Buckingham. 'Didn't you hear me? What about my reward?'

'Did you know a bard told me I wouldn't live long after I saw Richmond again?' Richard murmured. 'That's been playing on my mind a lot recently.'

'I'm sorry, my lord,' said Buckingham, his voice rising. 'But you promised...'

'Oh, for heaven's sake, Buckingham,' snarled Richard. 'You're like a clock that won't stop chiming. I can barely even think with you prattling on like that!'

'So, are you going to give me my reward, or not?' said Buckingham.

'Now you're *seriously* getting on my nerves,' said Richard, his face dark with anger. 'You may leave my presence. I'm definitely not in a giving mood today.'

Buckingham swept out. So that's how things were – treated with contempt after all he'd done, even making Richard King! But Richard was a dangerous man, and Buckingham had a distinct feeling that he might end up like Hastings if he wasn't careful. Maybe it was time to leave while he still had a head...

Things moved swiftly after that. Tyrrel murdered the Little Princes, although nobody knew exactly how, or where he buried them. But the people soon found out that the evil deed had been done, and they hated Richard all the more for it.

Buckingham fled to Wales, raised an army there, and marched on London.

'I'm more worried about Richmond than Buckingham,' Richard growled, stroking his chin and frowning when the news was brought to him. But then he suddenly smiled his wicked smile. He was a soldier, after all, and a good one, and this was something he knew how to deal with. 'Well, there's no point sitting around moaning. Call out my troops!' he yelled at his attendants, who jumped to his bidding. 'We must be swift and ruthless when traitors take the field!'

Richard ordered his forces in the west to move against Buckingham while he gathered an army in London. Before long, anvils were clanging as weapons were sharpened, captains and sergeants were shouting at their men, and the narrow streets echoed to the ringing of iron horseshoes on cobbles. It was all too familiar, of course. War was returning to the land like a dreaded ghost...

A few days later, Richard rode out of the palace leading his army, a great column of mounted knights and foot soldiers tramping along, armour glinting in the sun, weapons chinking. But they hadn't gone far before Richard held up his hand to halt the march. In front of him stood his mother and Queen Elizabeth.

'Tell me, you villain,' hissed Queen Elizabeth. 'Where are my babies? You should be branded a murderer, for you have killed my sons and my brothers.'

'Yes, and where is your brother Clarence, you toad?' hissed the duchess.

'Trumpeters, give me a blast to drown out these women,' snapped Richard. 'I'm King and I shouldn't have to listen to them and their stupid tittle-tattle.'

The trumpeters did as they were ordered, but the duchess ignored them. 'You're my son and you'll listen to me,' she said, moving closer to him.

'Oh, very well,' sighed Richard. 'But be brief, Mother. I'm in rather a hurry.'

'You're not going anywhere till I've finished,' said the duchess, pointing at him. 'These are the last words I shall ever speak to you. I lay upon you that most awful thing, a mother's curse, and I pray that your enemies will win. Your whole life has been full of shame and blood, and your death will be the same.' And with that, she turned and walked away, her head held high.

'I've got even more cause than she has to

curse you,' Elizabeth said quietly. 'But I'm not as good with words as your mother. So I'll just say amen to that.'

She turned to leave as well, but Richard dismounted and called her back.

'Stay a moment, Elizabeth,' he said. 'I need to have a word with you.'

'What do you want?' she said. 'I have no more sons here for you to kill.'

'Ah, but you do have a daughter,' said Richard, putting on the charm.

At first, Elizabeth was horrified to hear what Richard had in mind but, like Lady Anne, she soon came round to his way of thinking. The soldiers behind Richard nudged each other as they watched him work his evil magic.

Lady Elizabeth left eventually, saying that she would talk to him again.

'Stupid woman,' Richard muttered. Suddenly, two men rode up beside him and reined in their horses. It was Catesby and

Ratcliffe, another of Richard's men.

'My lord, a mighty fleet has appeared off our western coast,' Ratcliffe said breathlessly. 'It's Richmond and his army, and he plans to join Buckingham.'

'Oh, does he now, the villain,' said Richard, his eyes glowing with hatred. He started giving orders, sending fast riders out in every direction. Suddenly, his gaze fell on Lord Derby. 'And where are all your men, Derby?' he snapped.

'Er ... they're in the north, Your Majesty,' Derby muttered uncomfortably.

'They're not much use to me there, are they?' said Richard. 'You'd better get them to the west, and find some more, too. I know you want to join Richmond, and just to make sure you don't, I've ordered your son George to be taken as a hostage. The instant I hear you've betrayed me, his head will roll. Is that clear?'

'It is,' said a grim-faced Derby. 'Just be as true to him as I will be to you.'

Derby rode away, deep in thought, trying to work out how to help Richmond and save his son...

The army moved on, and later, when they had made camp, messenger after messenger came to Richard with tidings of more rebellions. It seemed that all over the country great men were rising against him and flocking to join the Earl of Richmond.

The next morning, a final messenger arrived.

'My lord, the army of Buckingham...' he began to say. But Richard couldn't take any more. He roared with anger and knocked the man down. 'Get out of here!' he screamed, and the man flinched. 'And don't come back until you can bring me some better news. I'm tired of hearing songs of death!'

'But, Your Majesty, the news I have is that Buckingham's army is defeated,' squeaked the messenger. 'And Lord Buckingham himself has been captured!'

Now Richard roared with pleasure, and did another of his little dances. He kept smiling even when he was told Richmond had landed. There was no time to rest, no time to delay. The final moment of truth was heading their way...

Act Five

Ghosts in the Night

Buckingham was beheaded that afternoon – a great event for him, of course, but a small one in the turmoil of war that had been unleashed. Two armies marched across the map of England like two bristling beasts, and finally met in the dead centre of the country, at Bosworth Field, near Leicester. There they pitched their tents and waited ... sniffing each other out, probing, searching for a weakness.

Richard stood before his tent, talking to his supporters and captains.

'Has anybody counted the traitors?' he said. 'How big is their army?'

'Six or seven thousand men at the most,' replied a knight, Lord Norfolk.

'Why, we have three times that many!' said Richard, laughing. 'Right, let's have a look at where we'll be fighting. Tomorrow is going to be a busy day.'

Richard strode off, followed by a gaggle of men.

A couple of miles away, Richmond was in his tent, listening to reports and giving orders to his captains.

'Our army might be small, but we're well prepared, and our cause is a just one,' he murmured to himself. 'Good Captain Blunt, where is Lord Derby?'

'He's with his regiment, my lord,' said Blunt. 'South of Richard's position.'

'I want you to take this note to him,' said Richmond, scribbling on a scroll.

'Don't worry, my lord, I'll make sure he gets it,' said Blunt, and hurried off.

Later, when Richmond was just settling down to sleep, a hooded man slipped into his tent. The man threw back his hood and Richmond saw it was Derby. They greeted each other warmly, and then Derby explained why he had come.

'I wish you victory in tomorrow's battle,' he said. 'And I'll do what I can to help. But I must be careful – Richard has taken my son

George hostage.'

They talked for a while longer, but eventually Derby returned to his soldiers.

'Leave me now, men,' Richmond said to his captains. 'I must try and get some sleep...' The tent emptied, and he was alone. He said a prayer, asking for victory in the battle to come, then settled down and closed his eyes.

Night had fallen on the two armies, the darkness dotted with the red lights of campfires, stars twinkling in the sky above. Guards kept watch, talking to each other in low voices, and soldiers on both sides slept fitfully, or lay awake, their minds full of fears about what the morning would bring. Richard had fallen asleep in his richly furnished tent and dozed untroubled, snoring gently.

Suddenly, a breeze rustled through the tops of the trees behind Richard's camp and swept through the tents, making the campfires snap and flicker. The sides of Richard's tent flapped and rippled, and he stirred uneasily in his sleep. He opened his eyes, and wondered for a second if he was dreaming. A strange figure stood before him, a man with a face as white as snow and blood running from gaping wounds all over his body. The man groaned and pointed at him.

'When I lived, you stabbed my body full of holes,' he wailed. 'Remember me tomorrow, for I am Henry the Sixth, the king you killed – then despair and die!'

The ghost vanished, and Richard drew in his breath sharply. It had certainly *looked* like the king he had killed, Henry of Lancaster. But it couldn't have been him, could it? So either he was dreaming, or it had been a ghost. Richard was just dismissing that idea when the breeze shook the tent once more, and a second strange figure appeared. Another man as white as snow with gaping wounds, but this one was wet, and drenched in red wine... It was Clarence!

'Remember me tomorrow,' Clarence groaned, 'and then despair and die...'

Richard whimpered, but there was no escape. Each of his victims came to visit him that night – Rivers, Grey and Vaughan, the Lady Anne, Hastings, Buckingham, even the Little Princes. And each of them pointed an accusing finger at him, and told him to remember them tomorrow during the battle – and then to despair and die. Richard closed his eyes at last, but his dreams were still full of blood and pain and screaming ... until he finally woke in a cold sweat. 'Sweet Jesus, have mercy!' he whispered, trembling and holding his head. 'It must have been a nightmare. So what is there to be afraid of? Myself, I suppose. I am a murderer, after all, and how awful it was to see in my dreams the people I have murdered, and hear them threatening me. It's almost enough to give me a conscience, to make me hate myself. And no one will pity me when I die...'

Just then, the tent flap flew open and Ratcliffe came bustling in. 'My lord, it's morning! Your friends are long since up and are buckling on their armour!'

'I had a terrible dream, Ratcliffe,' said Richard. 'And now I am afraid...'

'There's no point in being afraid of shadows, my lord,' said Ratcliffe.

'Well, those shadows have put more fear of death in me than Richmond and his whole army,' said Richard. But then he seemed to pull himself together. 'Come, I'll arm myself and go and check on the men, make sure they're true...'

Both armies were stirring in the morning light. Captains and sergeants shouted, horses neighed, men put on their armour and grabbed their weapons and hurried to their positions. Richmond emerged from his tent fully armed.

'Good morning, my lord,' said Captain Blunt. 'Did you sleep well?'

'I did,' said Richmond, smiling. 'It was the sweetest sleep, with the best dreams I've ever had. The souls of all the people Richard has murdered came to promise me victory, so my heart is full of joy. And now I'll address the troops.'

He climbed on his horse and rode along in front of the army, telling them again how just their cause was. 'I'll win this battle,' he said, 'or end the day a cold corpse. And if I win, I promise you we'll all share in the rewards of success. Now, sound the trumpets and advance! For God and St George! Onwards to victory!'

Richmond's men cheered, and the ground shook as they moved forward.

Richard was sitting on his horse as well, and had just finished speaking to his army. He was restored to his old self after the fears of the night, and his speech had been the usual combination of threats and promises nobody believed he would keep, all of it shot through with insults to Richmond and accusations of foul treachery. Now he turned slowly in his saddle and looked up at the sky.

'The sun will not be seen today,' he murmured. Dark clouds loomed over him, and a mist was swirling over the battlefield. 'The sky frowns on my army. But what do I care? It frowns on Richmond just as much on me... Norfolk, call Lord Derby, tell him to bring up his men. We'll have the archers in the middle of our line, with the knights on either flank. Well, what do you think, Norfolk?'

'It sounds like a good plan, my lord,' said Norfolk. And so the battle began...

The armies thundered across Bosworth Field and crashed together, two great beasts ripping and tearing at each other. Blades rose and fell, men roared and screamed and grunted, and blood stained the trampled grass dark red. Neither side yielded at first ... but then Richard saw his men being slowly pushed back.

'Where is Derby?' he yelled. 'He should have been here by now.'

'He says he won't help you, my lord,' replied Captain Blunt.

'What?' said Richard. 'Off with his son George's head, then!'

'That will have to wait until after the battle, my lord,' said Norfolk.

Richard knew he was right. They fought on, and before too long it was clear that Richard was losing. His army was crumbling before his eyes, and soon all he wanted was to find Richmond. He roamed all over the battlefield, calling on Richmond to fight him man to man, until at last his horse was killed under him.

Richard fell to the ground with a crash, but scrambled to his feet. 'A horse, a horse!' he screamed desperately. 'My kingdom for a horse!'

'Quickly, come with me, my lord,' said Catesby. 'I'll find you a horse.'

'Leave me alone, slave!' yelled Richard. 'There must be six Richmonds on this battlefield today. I've killed five already, but I'll find the real one yet!'

Suddenly the real Richmond *did* appear. He came charging out of the mist, his sword raised, roaring his war cry. Richard just had time to see him before Richmond swung his blade in a great sweeping arc, and cut off his head, golden crown and all. The battle was over, and Richard's remaining men surrendered.

'God and your courage be praised, victorious friends,' Richmond cried out as his men crowded round him. 'The day is ours – the evil tyrant is dead at last!'

A great cheer went up, and Richmond's men slapped each other on the back. Then Lord Derby appeared and pushed his way through the rejoicing throng.

'Here, brave Richmond, accept this,' he said, handing him Richard's crown. 'I plucked it from the head of your enemy. Wear it, enjoy it, and make much of it.'

'I thank you,' said Richmond, deeply moved. 'But tell me, is your son safe?'

'He is, my lord,' said Derby, smiling. 'Although I should call you Majesty, King Henry the Seventh. My son is in Leicester, where we should go now.'

'And that we will, good friend,' said Richmond. 'But first we must bury those who have died here, and give a pardon to the soldiers who fought for Richard, if they accept my authority. From this day onwards, we will unite the red rose and the white. England has long been mad and scarred herself with war. I swear those times are gone for good. The civil wars are over, and peace lives again.'

To which all the lords and captains and the army loudly cried, 'Amen!'

About the Author

Tony Bradman was born in London and still lives there. He has written a large number of books for children of all ages, including 25 titles about his most popular creation, Dilly the Dinosaur. Dilly the Dinosaur was made into a long-running TV series and one of the books was shortlisted for the Children's Book Award. Tony has also edited many anthologies of poetry and short stories.

Tony loves reading and going to see Shakespeare plays performed at the restored Globe Theatre on London's South Bank. He likes watching Shakespeare on film, too, and thinks the famous version of *Richard III* starring Laurence Olivier is one of the best Shakespeare films ever!

SHAKESPEARE TODAY

WILLIAM SHAKESPEARE'S

Macbeth

RETOLD BY
TONY BRADMAN

SHAKESPEARE TODAY

WILLIAM SHAKESPEARE'S

ROMEO & JULIET

RETOLD BY MICHAEL COX

SHAKESPEARE TODAY

WILLIAM
SHAKESPEARE'S

A Midsummer Night's Dream

RETOLD BY

ROBERT
SWINDELLS

SHAKESPEARE TODAY

William Shakespeare's

AS YOU LIKE IT

Retold by Jenny Oldfield